W9- BTC-209

Published in the United States of America by Star Bright Books, Inc.

The name Star Bright Books and the Star Bright Books logo are registered
trademarks of Star Bright Books, Inc. Please visit www.starbrightbooks.com.
For bulk orders, please email: orders@starbrightbooks.com,
or call: (617) 354-1300.

Hardback ISBN-13: 978-1-59572-104-4
Star Bright Books / MA / 00406160
Printed in China (WKT) 9 8 7 6 5 4

Paperback ISBN-13: 978-1-59572-185-3
Star Bright Books / MA / 00605170
Printed in China (WKT) 9 8 7 6

Elephant and genet copyright © Brian Wildsmith 1974.
Used with permission by Egmont UK Limited London.

Printed on paper from sustainable forests.

Library of Congress Cataloging-in-Publication Data

Wildsmith, Brian.
Brian Wildsmith's amazing animal alphabet.
p. cm.
ISBN 978-1-59572-104-4
1. Animals--Juvenile literature. 2. Alphabet books--Juvenile literature. I. Title.
II. Title: Amazing animal alphabet book.

QL49.W544 2007
590--dc22

2007033811

Brian Wildsmith's

Amazing ANIMAL
Alphabet

Star Bright Books

Cambridge Massachusetts

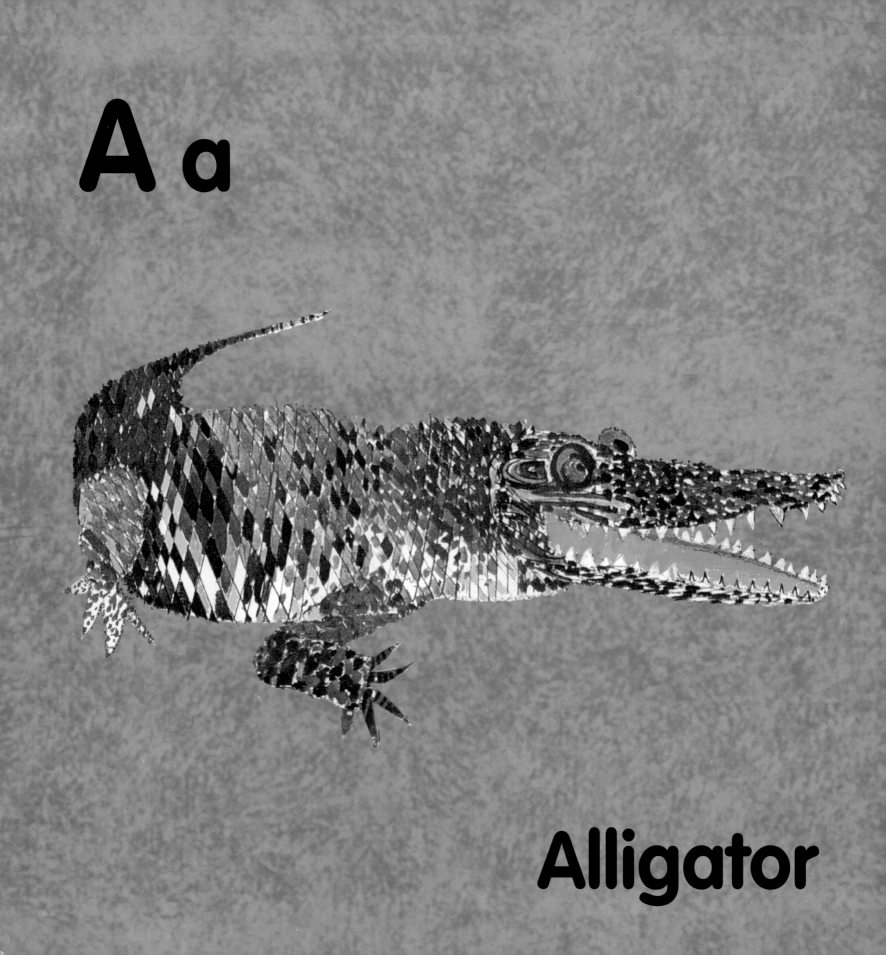

A a

Alligator

B b

Bear

C c

Camel

D d

Donkey

E e

Elephant

F f

Fox

G g

Genet

H h

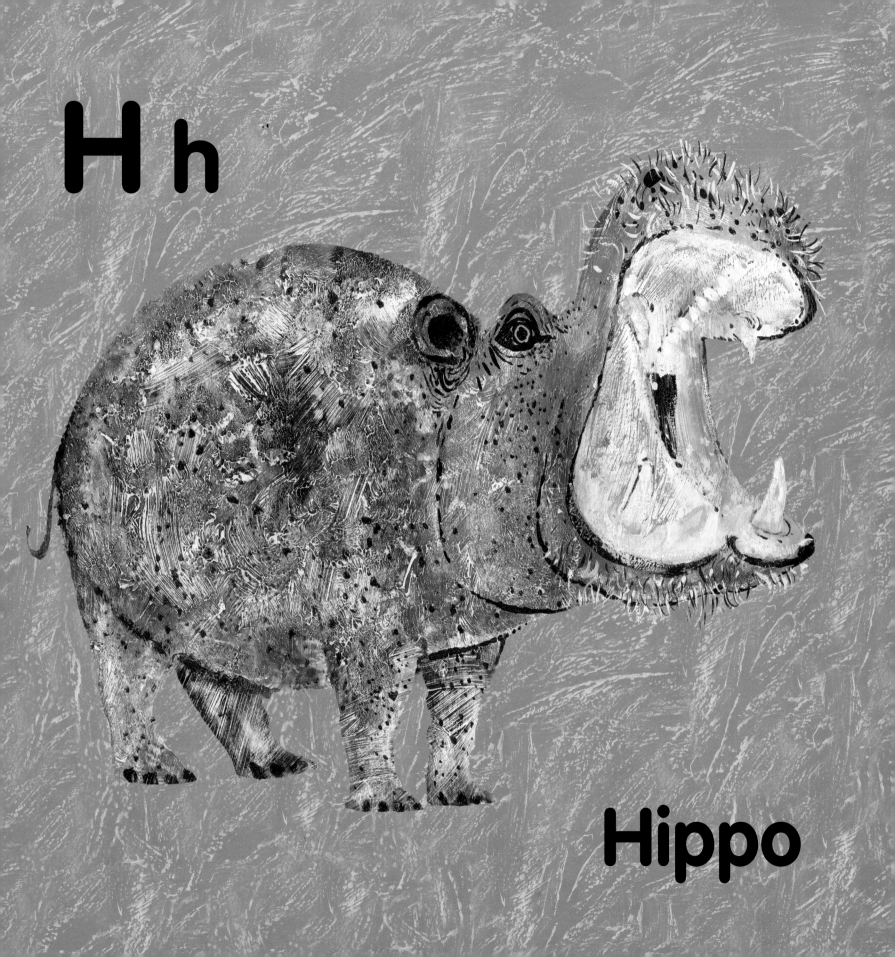

Hippo

I i

Ibex

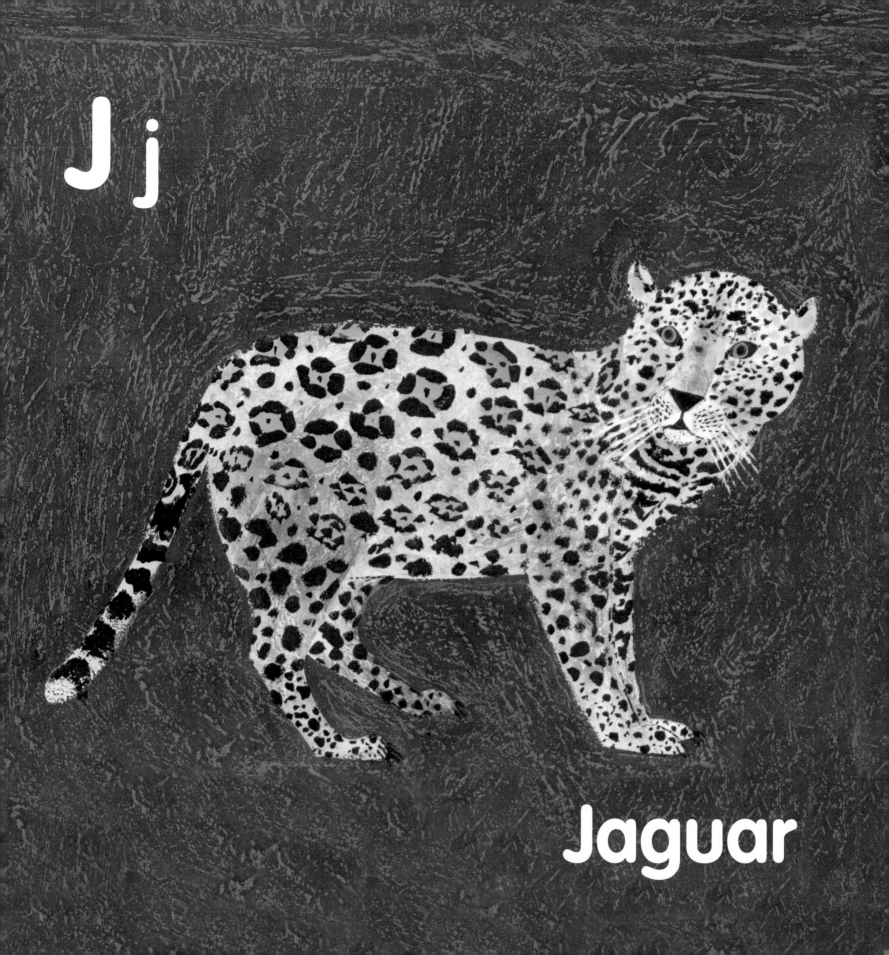

J j

Jaguar

K k

Kangaroo

Ll

Llama

M m

Mandrill

N n

Numbat

O o

Owl

P p

Platypus

Q q

Quetzal

R r

Reindeer

S s

Seal

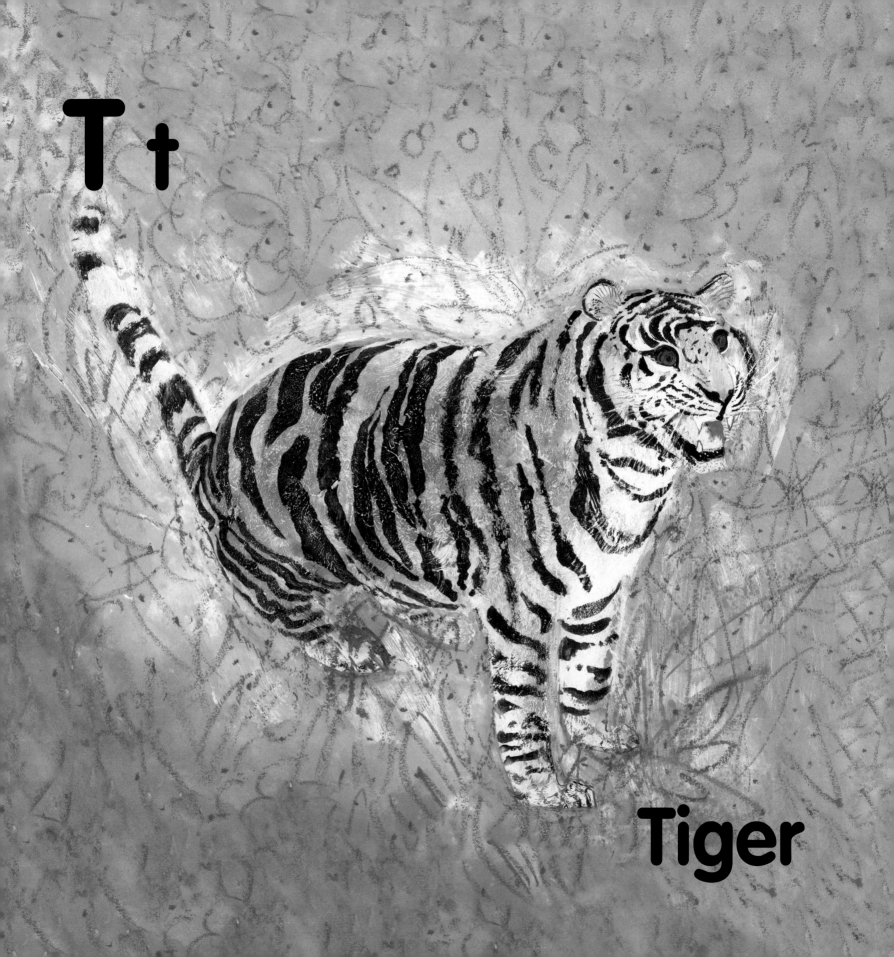

T t

Tiger

U u

Unau

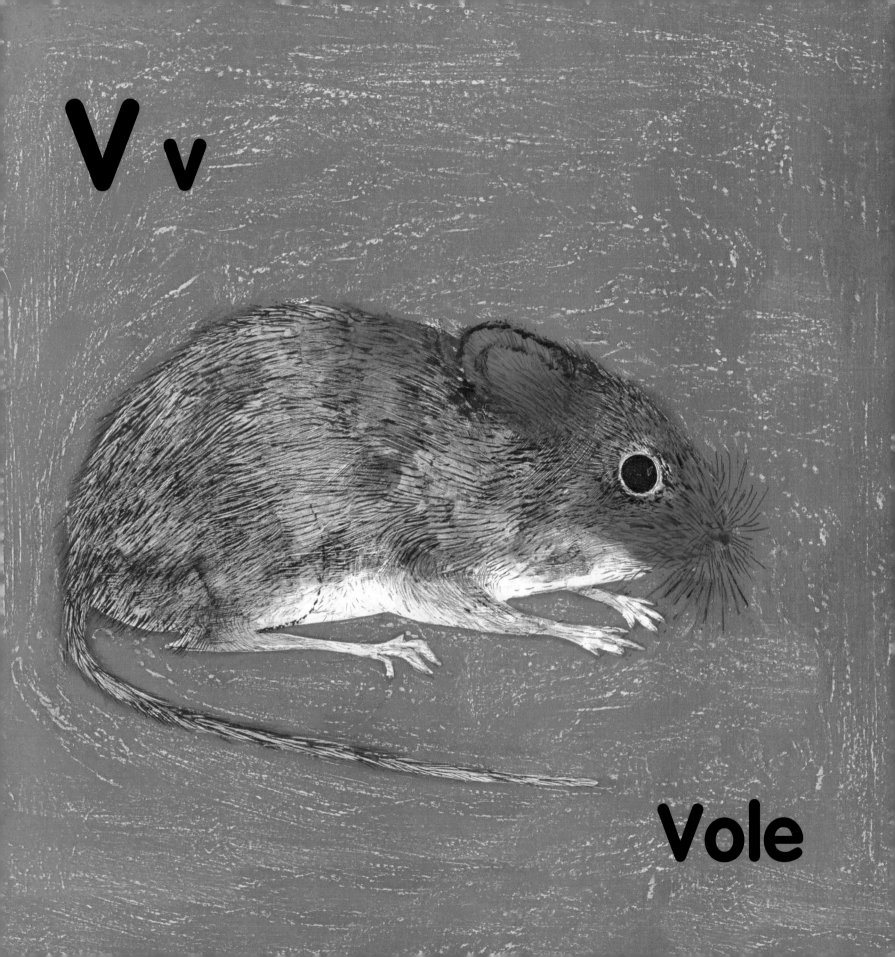

V v

Vole

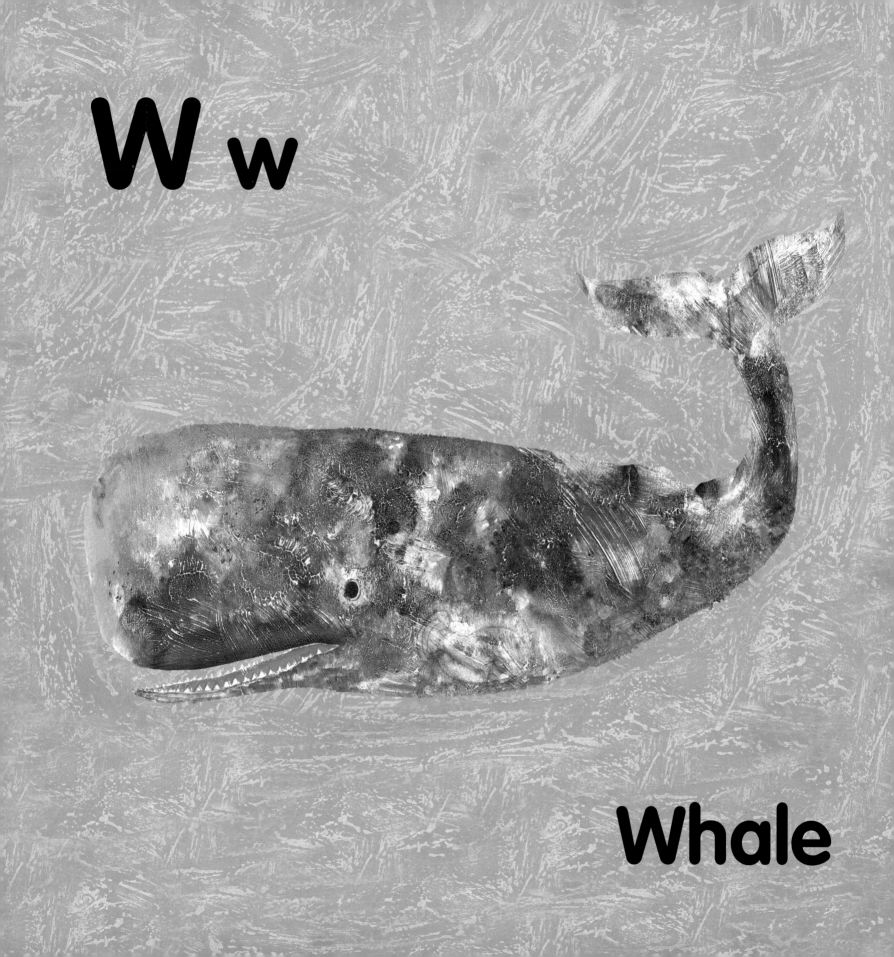

W w

Whale

X x

Xenops

Y y

Yak

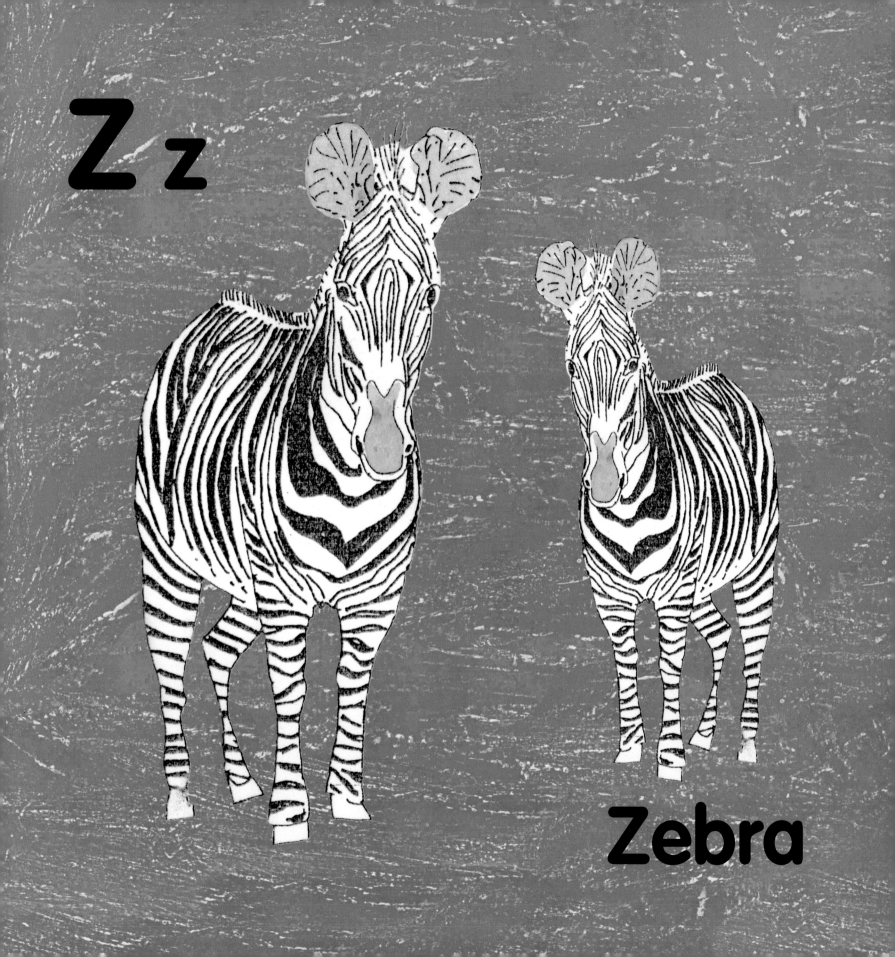

Z z

Zebra

Amazing Animal Facts

ALLIGATOR

Alligators are related to crocodiles. They live in lakes, swamps, and marshes in the United States and China. Alligators eat fish and animals, but rarely attack humans. Although they have over 75 teeth, they cannot chew, and they swallow their food whole.

BEAR

Bears are good climbers and swimmers. They have a very good sense of smell and will eat almost anything. Bears live in caves or burrows, and sleep through the winter living on the fat stored in their bodies. Baby bears are called cubs.

CAMEL

Camels live in the deserts of Asia and Africa. They are used for transport. Camels can go without food or water for six to seven days and then drink up to twenty gallons in ten minutes! Camels have one or two humps. Their humps store fat that nourishes them when needed.

DONKEY

Donkeys are related to horses, and can be ridden or used as pack animals. Donkeys have very long ears that are used to hear sounds from very far away. Their ears also help them to stay cool. The donkey's call is known as a bray.

ELEPHANT

Elephants are the largest land animals, and live in Africa and Asia. They eat 500 pounds of food a day! Elephants use their trunks for eating, drinking, bathing, and speaking. They have large ears, but their hearing is poor. The African elephant is larger than the Asian elephant.

FOX

Foxes live in many parts of the world and are often seen in cities. They belong to the same family as dogs and wolves, but are smaller and have bushy tails. Foxes live alone, and not in packs. They eat small animals, insects, fruit, and berries. A baby fox is called a kit.

GENET

Genets are found in Africa. They are very agile and can jump long distances from tree to tree. A genet's body will easily slide through a space only as big as its head. They hunt by stalking and pouncing on their prey. Like cats, genets purr, mew, and hiss.

HIPPO

Hippos live in Africa. They are the third-largest mammal. Hippos spend most of the day in water with just their nostrils and eyes above water. They can stay completely under water for about six minutes. Hippos are very aggressive. Despite their size they can run very fast.

IBEX

Ibex, also called steinbocks, are mountain goats. They live in the mountains of Europe, Central Asia, and North Africa. Their large horns keep growing throughout their lives. Male ibex horns can grow to three feet or more, but the female's horns grow to only about fifteen inches.

JAGUAR

Jaguars are solitary animals found in the tropical rainforests of South America. They have powerful bodies and are skilled at climbing and swimming. They hunt their prey by stalking and ambushing. Jaguars are closely related to lions, tigers, and leopards.

KANGAROO

Kangaroos live in Australia. They have powerful hind legs that enable them to hop in great leaps. They can travel as fast as forty miles per hour for short distances. Kangaroos eat grass and can go for months without water. Females carry their young, called joeys, in belly pouches.

LLAMA

Llamas are members of the camel family, and live in the high mountains of South America. They are used as pack animals. Llamas get the moisture they need from shrubs and plants. They give birth standing up. A baby llama is called a cria.

MANDRILL

Mandrills are the world's largest monkeys. They live in large groups in the tropical rainforests of the Congo and Guinea in Africa. Male mandrills have brightly colored faces and bottoms. Their color becomes brighter as they get older. They eat small animals, plants, and insects.

NUMBAT

Numbats, also called banded anteaters, are about the size of rats. They eat termites and have long sticky tongues that can stretch to half the length of their bodies. They live in southwestern Australia and carry their babies on their backs.

OWL

Owls are found worldwide. They sleep during the day and hunt at night. Thick feathers help to muffle the sound of their wings when they fly. Owls have very good eyesight and can see long distances even in poor light. They can turn their heads in almost a full circle to see behind them.

PLATYPUS

Platypuses live in pairs in simple burrows in the bank of rivers and streams of Australia. They lay eggs and produce milk to feed their babies. They have broad, flat tails and five-toed webbed feet. The male platypus produces venom that can kill small animals.

QUETZAL

Quetzals are found in Central America and are considered one of the most beautiful birds in the world. They nest in the hollows of rotting trees and both parents take turns sitting on the eggs and feeding the young. They eat fruit and insects. The quetzal is the national bird of Guatemala.

REINDEER

Reindeer live in the Arctic and sub-Arctic regions. They have broad hooves that spread out when they walk on snow or on swampy ground. Both males and females grow new antlers every year. Reindeer are used to transport, feed, and clothe people. Reindeer are also known as caribou.

SEAL

Most seals live near the Arctic and Antarctic, but some live in warmer areas. Seals can stay under water for as long as thirty minutes, but must then surface for air. They even do this in their sleep. Seals use their flippers to move along the ground. Baby seals are called pups.

TIGER

Tigers are the biggest animals in the cat family. They live in Asia and are endangered. Tigers can run very fast and are good swimmers. They spend a lot of time in water. They are not good tree climbers and have difficulty climbing down. Baby tigers are called cubs.

UNAU

Unaus are two-toed sloths. They have long, curved claws that enable them to hang from tree branches in the rainforests of Central and South America. They sleep for fifteen to eighteen hours each day and move so slowly that a few paces is often the journey of a whole week.

VOLE

Voles are mouse-like animals that live in underground tunnels. They are about three to four inches long and are found almost everywhere. Voles eat grass, seeds, leaves, bulbs, and the roots and bark of small trees. They rarely live longer than a year.

WHALE

Whales are the largest animals on the planet. Although they live in water, they are warm-blooded, breathe through lungs, and feed their young milk. They have blowholes on top of their heads that help them breathe in air even when they are submerged under water.

XENOPS

Xenopses are small birds that live in tree hollows in Central and South America. They eat insects found in decaying trees. Male and female xenopses build their nest together. Both parents take turns feeding and keeping babies warm after they are born.

YAK

Yaks are humped animals found in Central Asia. Wild yaks are bigger than domestic yaks and live in herds. Yaks have long, shaggy coats that are used to make yarn. Yak dung is burned for heat and cooking.

ZEBRA

Zebras are found in eastern and southern Africa. They live in family groups and recognize each other by their striped pattern, which, like a fingerprint, is unique to each animal. The zebra's beauty lies in the amazing regularity of the alternate black-and-white stripes that cover its body.